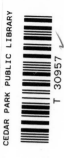

Thomas Tuttle, Just in Time

BECKY THOMAN LINDBERG
Illustrations by NANCY POYDAR

ALBERT WHITMAN & COMPANY
Morton Grove, Illinois

Library of Congress Cataloging-in-Publication Data

Lindberg, Becky Thoman.
Thomas Tuttle, just in time / Becky Thoman Lindberg;
illustrated by Nancy Poydar.
p. cm.
Summary: Thomas Tuttle has lots of trouble
working on special projects for his third-grade class.
ISBN 0-8075-7898-3
[1. Schools—Fiction.] I. Poydar, Nancy, ill. II. Title.
PZ7.L65716Th 1994   93-38606
[Fic]—dc20   AC   CIP

To my son, Peter Lindberg.

Contents

»1«

Thomas Takes A Chance

Thomas Tuttle looked at the T-shirt he'd just pulled out from under his bed. Was it clean enough to wear to school? "How about this one?" he asked his friend Arthur Wilmot.

"Nope," said Arthur. "Too muddy."

Thomas found another shirt on the floor behind his desk. He started to put it on.

But Arthur shook his head. "Too greasy."

Then Thomas noticed his favorite blue sweatshirt hanging from the bedpost. He held it up and saw that one sleeve was smeared with sticky pink stuff. Bubblegum, maybe?

"Uh-uhh," said Arthur.

"I know." Thomas sighed. "Too gooey."

There was only one place left to look for something to wear. He dug into his laundry hamper.

Dirty clothes flew everywhere as he tossed them out of his way. A tube sock sailed over his shoulder and landed on Arthur's head.

"Aaagh!" Arthur snatched it off and threw it on the floor.

Thomas pulled a red T-shirt out of the hamper. There was a spaghetti sauce stain down the front, but the smudge didn't show up much against the background. Yeah, he decided, it'll do.

Arthur went to the window and looked up and down the street. "There goes old Chelsea-Delsea. Maybe we'd better get going."

"Don't worry," said Thomas. "She always leaves early."

Arthur pointed to a coffee can sitting on the windowsill. "Hey, what happened to your plant?"

Mrs. Findlay's class had grown bean plants at school. After that science unit, the third graders were allowed to take the plants home.

Thomas shrugged. "I don't know."

"Well, it looks pretty awful." Arthur poked at the dry dirt in the coffee can. "It'll never get big enough to have beans growing on it."

That was all right with Thomas. He didn't even like green beans.

Arthur stared at the plant. "I think it's almost dead. You've murdered a helpless vegetable."

Thomas reached for the coffee can. "Let me see." He touched one of the limp leaves. "I guess you're right. I should've watered it more."

Arthur stuck his face up close to the plant. "How're you feeling, little fellow? Not too good, huh?"

"Oh, brother," Thomas muttered. "I can't believe you're talking to a plant."

Arthur shrugged. "Why shouldn't I?"

Thomas tugged the red T-shirt over his head. "Because plants aren't people, that's why. They can't talk back."

"Dogs and cats can't speak," Arthur said, "and people talk to them all the time."

"That's different," Thomas said. "Dogs and cats are almost like people. They even have names. You didn't give your bean plant a name, did you?"

Arthur nodded. "Uh-huh."

"You did?" Thomas stared at Arthur. "What did you name it?"

"I call my plant Spot."

"But that's a dog's name."

"Yeah!" said Arthur. "That's what I like about it. My parents still won't let me have a pooch,"—his mouth turned down—"so I gave a dog's name to my plant."

"At least you have your two goldfish."

Arthur smiled. "Good old Ed and Ralph."

Thomas smoothed the dirt around the bean's skinny stem. Maybe naming a plant wasn't so dumb. If Arthur could do it, so could he.

He said, "I'm going to call my plant . . . Lucky."

Arthur glanced at the coffee can and shook his head. "He doesn't seem very lucky to me."

"I know," Thomas said. "But from now on, I'm going to take care of him." He got a cup of water from the bathroom and poured it over the plant.

Arthur said, "We'd better get going." He heaved his backpack onto his shoulder and picked up a paper shopping bag.

"What's in the bag?" asked Thomas.

"My solar system project," Arthur said.

Thomas stared at him in alarm.

"I made a model of Saturn," Arthur said proudly, "out of toothpicks and styrofoam peanuts."

Thomas said, "Are you telling me the solar system project is due today?"

"Yeah." Arthur stopped, his hand on the doorknob. "Don't you have a project?"

Thomas collapsed in a chair. "No! I forgot."

"Uh-oh!" Arthur glanced at the clock on Thomas's nightstand. "You only have two minutes to come up with an idea."

"I know." Thomas looked wildly around the room. He yanked at his dark, springy hair.

Then he snapped his fingers. He *did* have something that might work. He jumped out of his chair and started digging through a plastic crate full of sports equipment.

"Okay," he said, as he snatched up an orange

ball made of foam. "I'm ready."

"What are you gonna do with that?" asked Arthur.

"Use it for my project, of course."

Arthur shook his head. "That isn't a solar system project. That's a Nerf ball."

"You don't understand." Thomas held the ball in the palm of his hand. "This is the red planet— Mars."

He tore out a few little bits of foam. "See, these are craters on the planet's surface."

Arthur shrugged. "I don't think Mrs. Findlay's gonna fall for it."

Thomas really didn't think so either. "What do you expect when I only had two minutes!"

"Actually, she gave us three weeks to do this project."

"Yeah, I know," Thomas said sheepishly. He tossed the foam ball into the air. "It's worth a try," he said as they walked out the door.

»2«

Not Again!

Thomas glanced up at Mrs. Findlay and then ducked his head. Uh-oh, he thought. She's getting ready to call on another person.

Soon he would have to get up in front of the whole class and show his project. His Nerf ball idea seemed worse and worse every minute.

"Who wants to be next?" said Mrs. Findlay. "How about . . ."

Don't pick me, Thomas pleaded silently. Puh-leeze, anybody but me!

"Chelsea," said Mrs. Findlay.

Thomas smiled. Chelsea Martin walked quickly to the front of the room, her straight brown hair swinging with each step. "My project is a report on the planet Venus," she announced.

While Chelsea read, Thomas stared at the big, round wall clock. If her report is long enough, he told himself, there won't be time for anyone else.

But she stopped reading after a few minutes. Thomas felt cheated; was she finished already?

Not quite. "Here's a picture," Chelsea said. She held up a drawing of Venus, done with colored pencils.

"Very good," said Mrs. Findlay. As she marked her grade book, Thomas glanced enviously at Arthur.

Arthur had already presented his project. He slouched comfortably in his chair, his long legs sticking straight out in front of him.

"All right," said Mrs. Findlay. "Who's next?"

Thomas held his breath.

In front of him, Beverly Ann strained forward in her seat. She waved her arm back and forth, up and down, and sideways.

What does that girl think she is? Thomas asked himself crossly. A windmill?

Mrs. Findlay smiled. "Okay, Beverly Ann. You seem eager for your turn—go ahead."

Beverly Ann smoothed her long blonde hair. "At last," she murmured.

Thomas looked at the empty chair in front of him. Now it was going to be even harder to hide from the teacher.

He fumbled in his desk and pulled out his spelling workbook. While Beverly Ann unrolled a large poster, he propped up the book in front of him. Then he slid down in his seat.

"Ahem!" said Beverly Ann, trying to get everyone's attention. "This is the *entire* solar system."

Thomas peeked around his spelling book. Beverly Ann was pointing to an ugly yellow blob in the center of her poster.

"See, here's the sun," she said. "And those other things are the planets." After talking about the solar system for a few more minutes, she stopped to take a breath.

"Good work," said Mrs. Findlay.

"And—" Beverly Ann looked around to make sure everyone was listening. "I finished my project a whole week early."

Mrs. Findlay smiled. "Great! What a good worker."

"Humph!" said Thomas under his breath.

Mary Lynne Woodlie raised her hand to go next. Her project was a lumpy, bumpy model of the moon's surface made from homemade salt-and-flour paste.

A few more people presented their projects. Then Mrs. Findlay said, "I think we're just about finished." She bent over her grade book and ran her finger down the page.

Immediately, Beverly Ann's hand shot into the air. Out of her mouth came little noises. "Oooh! Oooh!"

Mrs. Findlay looked up. "Yes, Beverly Ann?"

"I know who hasn't had a turn yet."

She means me, thought Thomas. His heart began to thud.

Mrs. Findlay looked at Beverly Ann. "Who?"

"It's Thomas." Beverly Ann turned halfway around in her chair to smirk at him.

"Oh, that's right," said Mrs. Findlay. "Thomas?

Are you there behind that book?"

Reluctantly, Thomas laid down his spelling workbook. "Uh-huh."

"Then pay attention, please. It's your turn." Mrs. Findlay paused. "You do have a project, don't you?"

"Well . . . yeah."

Slowly, Thomas got to his feet. As he plodded up the aisle to the front of the room, he could feel everyone watching him. It was a lonely, uncomfortable feeling.

Thomas reached into the pocket of his jeans and pulled out his Nerf ball. "This is my project."

The classroom was quiet. Everyone stared at Thomas and the thing he held in his hand.

"Hmmmm," said Mrs. Findlay with a frown. "What is it supposed to be?"

"Uh—" Thomas swallowed. He was having a hard time talking. But finally, he managed to get the words out. "It's the planet Mars."

He glanced sideways at Mrs. Findlay. She didn't often get angry at her students. But now there was a crease between her eyebrows, and her lips were pressed tightly together, like two sides of a zipper.

She motioned to Thomas. "Bring your project here."

While Thomas stood by her desk, Mrs. Findlay inspected the ball. She pressed her thumbs into the soft foam. She held it up to the light.

Finally, she handed it back. "Thomas, I'm afraid this isn't good enough. It's not third-grade work."

Thomas shifted from one foot to the other and looked at the floor. "But I made those craters—"

"You may sit down now," Mrs. Findlay said.

Thomas slunk back to his seat. Mrs. Findlay went to the blackboard and started to go over the spelling words.

"Psst!" Arthur whispered. "Tough luck!"

"I know," said Thomas. "But it was worth a—"

"Thomas and Arthur!" Mrs. Findlay gave them a stern look. "What have I told you about whispering? Come up here—both of you—and write your names on the blackboard."

"Awww! Not again!" Arthur muttered.

Thomas heaved a big sigh. If he got in trouble

two more times—if he got two check marks after his name—he would have to visit the principal.

He dragged himself up to the blackboard and printed his name in teeny, tiny letters. His name was on the board, all right. But he hoped that no one would be able to read it.

» 3 «

The Wrong Side

When it was time for morning recess, Mrs. Findlay's third graders hurried out the back door of the school. Arthur had to stop to tie his shoe, and Thomas waited for him. They both wound up at the tail end of the line.

"Hey," said Arthur. "It's nice out, isn't it?"

"Huh?" Thomas had been slogging along with his head down. He glanced up at the cloudless blue sky. "It's okay, I guess."

Arthur leaned close to Thomas and stared into his face. "What's wrong with you?"

Thomas shrugged. "I feel kind of bad."

"Are you going to be sick?" asked Arthur.

"Wait a minute. Let me get out of the way!" He leaped back a few feet.

Thomas shook his head. "It's not that sort of feeling."

He kicked a pebble across the blacktop. "I just wish I could get through one day without getting my name on the blackboard."

"Me, too," Arthur said. "Mrs. Findlay should give someone else a chance."

"That's not all," Thomas said. "She keeps assigning projects, and mine is always the worst."

"Yeah. You'll probably get a *D*." Arthur grinned. "You know, *D* for dog doo-doo!"

Thomas frowned. "I hope not."

"Aw, forget about it," Arthur said. "Come on, let's go play kickball."

When they got to the field, the game had already started. Thomas and Arthur headed for the line of third graders waiting to kick the ball.

Thomas watched Charlie Rivera hurl the ball in a straight line toward Aaron Wrexroad. Then—

"Oooph!" He felt a sharp pain in his foot. Somebody had just tramped on it.

He whirled around. It was Beverly Ann. Without saying anything, she pushed right in front of him.

"Hey, wait a minute!" Thomas said.

Arthur crossed his arms on his chest. "Hey, Beverly Ann!"

"Excuse me." Chelsea Martin shoved past the boys.

Thomas looked at Arthur. "What's going on?"

"Excuse me," said Abigail MacCready.

"Please get out of the way," said Mary Lynne Woodlie. The girls elbowed their way ahead of Thomas and Arthur.

Arthur's face was red. "You can't get in front of us like that!"

"Yes, we can," said Mary Lynne. "You're not even supposed to be here."

"You can't join the team now," Chelsea said. "The game's already started."

Beverly Ann tossed her head. "You were late, so it's your own fault. The early bird gets the bug."

"You mean worm," Thomas said.

Beverly Ann frowned. "The early worm gets

the bug? That doesn't make sense."

Thomas shook his head. "No, I mean—"

"He means dirt," Arthur interrupted. "The worm gets the dirt."

"You've all got it wrong," said Abigail. "The saying goes, 'Two birds in a bush are better than one.'"

"Why?" demanded Arthur. "If they're in a bush, a cat can catch them. It's better for birds to be in the sky. Or at least in a tree."

Abigail seemed confused. "But—"

"Some birds eat seeds," Chelsea said. "But some eat worms. That's what the saying is all about."

Arthur said, "Yeah, it's like dinosaurs. Some of them eat meat and some eat plants."

Mary Lynne shook her head. "I don't understand what dinosaurs have to do with being late."

Arthur shrugged. "Don't ask me. Beverly Ann's the one who started the whole thing."

"What!" said Beverly Ann.

Thomas glanced at her scowling face. "Come on, Arthur," he said. "Let's get outta here. We can swing on the tire swing."

"Okay," Arthur said. "We're going now," he told the girls. "Don't try to talk us out of it."

Ten minutes later, recess was over. When the third graders got back to their classroom, Mrs. Findlay picked up a stack of papers. She began walking around the room, placing a paper face-down on each desk.

Thomas got Arthur's attention. "What's she passing out?" he whispered.

Someone in the next row had already turned over his paper. Arthur craned his neck so he could see it. "The grades for the solar system project."

"Oh." Thomas wondered what grade he would get. He tapped his front teeth with his pen.

Plop! Mrs. Findlay dropped a sheet of looseleaf paper on his desk and moved on. Thomas stared at it nervously.

Lifting a tiny corner of the paper, he peeked underneath. He could see something red, part of a letter scrawled on the page, but he couldn't make it out.

He lifted the paper a little higher. The part of

the letter he could see didn't have the right shape for a *C*. Maybe Arthur was right. Maybe Mrs. Findlay had given him a *D*. Thomas sighed. *D* for dog doo-doo.

He pulled a little more of the paper up and peeked at it again. Wait a minute—the letter didn't have the right shape for a *D*, either.

Taking a deep breath, Thomas flipped the paper over. Oh no! His grade was worse than a *D;* it was an *E*! *E* for ENORMOUS mistake! He crumpled the sheet into a ball and stuffed it inside his desk.

Mrs. Findlay had finished passing out the grades.

"Some people did very well on the solar system project," she said with a smile.

She moved to the far end of the blackboard. With a piece of yellow chalk, she drew a huge star.

"All of these people got *A*'s," she said and began to call out names. "Lucy Burnett, Katie Klein, Chelsea Martin . . . ."

Mrs. Findlay wrote the names of the *A* students on the blackboard, right beneath the yellow star. It seemed to Thomas that the list went on and on.

Down at the other end of the board was the list of students who'd misbehaved that day. That's where his name was.

While Mrs. Findlay had her back turned, Arthur swiveled around in his seat. "Hey, Thomas," he whispered, "we're on the wrong side of the blackboard."

"I know," Thomas said with a sigh. "I know."

»4«

Arthur's Fish Formula

Saturday morning Thomas woke up early, and one of the first things he did was check on his bean plant. Lucky stirred a little in the breeze coming through the open window. Then one of his leaves dropped off.

Thomas looked at his plant in dismay. After a moment, he went downstairs to find some help.

His mother had already left for her job at the hospital. But Mr. Tuttle was in the basement, knee-deep in dirty clothes.

Thomas stepped carefully between the mounds of soiled laundry dotting the floor. "Hey, Dad, what do plants need to be really healthy?"

Mr. Tuttle stuffed clothes into the washing machine. "Well, let me see. Water and plant food, I guess. But not too much." He sighed as he patted his protruding stomach. "Just like people, plants shouldn't be overfed."

"What else?" Thomas asked.

"Light, and good soil."

"Oh, I see. Thanks, Dad." Thomas went out to the garage to see if he could find any plant food.

He was rummaging through the cartons and bottles on the shelves when he heard a tap on the window. There was Arthur, his nose pressed against the glass. "What's up?" he asked after Thomas let him in.

Thomas said, "I'm trying to find some plant food for Lucky."

"How about that stuff?" Arthur pointed to a can which had a picture of lush pink flowers on its label.

"That's rose food," said Thomas. "Do you think that'll work?"

"I don't know," said Arthur. "Lucky might get confused."

"You mean he might try to grow pink beans or something?"

"Yeah," said Arthur. "You'd better not risk it."

Thomas sighed. "I guess I should get some real vegetable fertilizer." He shook his head sadly. "I've got about three dollars left from my allowance this month. But I was saving it."

"Saving it? For what?"

Thomas shrugged. "I haven't decided. But something good—not fertilizer."

Arthur said, "I have some plant food you can use."

"Really?"

"Yeah. My goldfish are always making it for me."

"Aw, come on. How can goldfish make plant food?"

"Easy. Every time I put fresh water in their bowl, I save the old water. It's supposed to be good for plants."

"Really?"

"Yeah, it's good stuff. I already have a couple bucketfuls I'm keeping in the basement."

Thomas wasn't sure smelly old fish water was something he'd like to have around the house.

"I'm thinking of selling it door to door," said Arthur.

"I guess I could give it a try." Thomas went to ask his father about going over to Arthur's.

"It's okay," Thomas said when he got back. "Let's go."

The Wilmots had a big old Victorian house. When they got there, Arthur pointed to some bedraggled plants. "See those daffodils? I've been feeding them my fish water."

"Oh." Thomas didn't think the flowers looked too healthy.

Arthur said, "I can't understand why they aren't getting bigger." He got down on his hands and knees to study the daffodils.

"Mom won't like it if her flowers die," he said in a worried voice. "I'd better go get some more fish water."

He came back in a few minutes, carrying a bucket.

"Pee-u!" said Thomas after catching a whiff.

"Fertilizer is supposed to smell like that," said Arthur.

He tilted the bucket and dumped a stream of greenish liquid over the flowers. "There! That'll fix 'em up."

Thomas watched the fish water soak into the ground. Who knows, he thought, maybe it'll help.

All at once—zhuuup! One of the daffodils sagged.

Then another went limp, and another. Soon, all the flowers were as droopy as a group of children sitting in a dentist's waiting room.

"Oh no!" Arthur stared at the daffodils. "You don't think the fish formula did that, do you?"

"Well-l-l-l," said Thomas. "Maybe."

"What am I gonna do?"

"I don't know." Thomas thought a minute. "Maybe you could plant new flowers."

"Yeah!" said Arthur. "I can buy some daffodils at Dipple's Dime Store. Mom will never know the difference!"

Arthur went into the house to get his money. When he came out again, he had a sheepish expression. A small girl with sandy-colored hair like Arthur's was by his side.

Thomas said, "Your sister's not coming along, is she?"

"Yeah."

"Why?" Thomas didn't want a four-year-old tagging after them, especially one dressed like this. Clip-on earrings sparkled on her ears, while a pair of large sunglasses kept sliding down her nose. Though it was only March, she wore a T-shirt, shorts, and pink flip-flops on her bare feet.

"Lizzie was looking out the window," said Arthur. "If we don't take her with us, she'll tell Mom about the daffodils."

"Tattletale!" said Thomas, scornfully.

Lizzie made a face at Thomas. "You have to take me to the store." She pushed up her sun-glasses. "So there!"

"Oh, all right." Thomas pointed to Lizzie's flip-flops. "But you'd better change your shoes. It's five blocks to the store."

Lizzie shook her head. "No! I like these."

Arthur shrugged. "Okay, but you've got to keep

up with us." He motioned to Thomas. "Come on, let's go."

At first, Thomas and Arthur were walking side-by-side, with Lizzie trailing a few feet behind. But soon, Lizzie ran around and got in front.

"I want to be the leader," she said. She trotted along with her shoes slapping her heels at every step. *Thwack-thwack, thwack-thwack.*

Thomas and Arthur exchanged a look, but neither said anything. Thomas didn't think Lizzie would be able to keep up that pace all the way to the store.

Sure enough, after they'd walked a block, Lizzie's footsteps got slower. Then she began to lag behind.

"Arthur," she said plaintively, "can you carry me piggyback?"

"No!" Arthur said. "You're too heavy."

Lizzie didn't say anything, but Thomas heard a sniff.

"Just ignore her," whispered Arthur.

"Okay," said Thomas.

Lizzie plodded along behind them, the sound of

her sniffles mixing with the noises made by her shoes. *Thwack*! . . . sniffle. *Thwack*! . . . sniffle. *Thwack*! . . . sniffle—

The sounds stopped, and Thomas and Arthur turned around to see what was going on. Lizzie was about ten feet behind them, sitting cross-legged on the sidewalk. "Unless you carry me," Lizzie said, "I'm gonna stay right here."

"Oh, come on, Lizzie," said Arthur. "It's just three more blocks. You can walk that far."

"No!" Lizzie shook her head. "I'm tired, and these flip-flops make my toes hurt."

"I told you to change your shoes," said Thomas. "But you wouldn't listen."

Lizzie took off her flip-flops. "Here," she said. "I don't want them anymore."

"Don't be silly," said Arthur. "Come on."

"No! I'm not moving!" screeched Lizzie. "Never, ever, ever—"

Arthur turned to Thomas. "Now what are we gonna do?"

»5«

A Mean Man

While Lizzie sat screeching, Thomas considered. "Why don't we just leave her here and pick her up on the way back?"

Arthur shook his head. "What if something happens to her? I'm the one"—he thumped his chest— "who'll get blamed."

Lizzie had stopped yelling so that she could listen to their conversation. "Yeah!" she said.

Thomas looked up and down the street. A few younger children were playing in their yards. Katie Klein's pigtailed sister, Pamela, was hauling a large wagon back and forth on the sidewalk in front of her house.

"I know!" Thomas snapped his fingers. "Let's see if we can borrow that wagon. Then we can pull Lizzie to the store."

Pamela agreed to lend them the wagon after Lizzie said she could borrow her flip-flops. "We'll bring it back in half an hour," said Thomas.

Arthur motioned to his sister. "Get in there, Lizzie."

Lizzie pushed up her sunglasses. With a big grin on her face, she scrambled into the wagon.

Thomas and Arthur took turns pulling it. The wagon bounced and rattled over the sidewalk cracks, but Lizzie didn't seem to mind.

When they reached Dipple's Dime Store, Thomas stepped on the black runner that made the automatic door open. Arthur pulled the wagon into the store.

"Hey, kids!" The security guard, who had been lounging against a wall inside, stood up straight. "You can't bring that wagon in here."

The guard made a shooing motion with his hand. "Go ahead, take it back outside."

Thomas whispered, "We have to do it."

"I know," said Arthur. They turned the wagon around and pulled it through the double doors.

Lizzie hopped out. "I don't like that man."

"I don't either," said Arthur impatiently. "But what're we gonna do now? We can't leave the wagon out here. Someone might take it."

Thomas thought it was too bad the wagon wasn't a horse. Then they could tie it to a hitching post.

He said, "There's nothing else we can do. I guess we'll just have to chance it."

Arthur shrugged. "Okay," he said. They left the wagon outside, and they all went back inside the store.

The security guard was still standing by the door. "Wait a minute." He shook his head at Lizzie. "She can't come in here," he said, and pointed to a sign: NO BARE FEET ALLOWED.

"What's that man talking about?" Lizzie whispered.

"You're not allowed in the store because you have bare feet," Arthur said glumly.

Lizzie burst into tears.

Thomas was embarrassed. But at the same time, he didn't think the rule was fair. What if a person didn't have any shoes? What if he were coming to the store to buy them, and then he couldn't get in?

It didn't make sense.

Arthur had grabbed Lizzie's hand. "Come on," he said as he led her to the door.

But Lizzie broke free. She dashed over to the guard.

"I think you're mean!" she said, and she kicked him in the shin.

Thomas gasped.

Arthur twisted the bottom of his T-shirt. "She's only four years old," he blurted out. "She didn't mean it!"

Lizzie scowled. "I did, too, mean it!"

"Oh . . . it's all right," said the security guard. Tugging at his shirt collar, he glanced around uneasily.

Arthur pulled Lizzie by the arm. "Let's go," he whispered, "before he changes his mind and throws us all in jail."

Looking a little frightened, Lizzie allowed herself to be led outside. She started to pace back and forth on the sidewalk while she muttered rude things about the guard. "I bet his feet smell . . . I bet he picks his nose . . ."

"Would you stay out here with Lizzie?" Arthur asked Thomas. "Then I can go back in the store and buy the daffodils."

"Okay," said Thomas. He sat on the curb a few feet away from Lizzie.

Thomas thought about his bean plant. After what had happened to Mrs. Wilmot's daffodils, he wasn't interested in trying Arthur's fish formula. He wondered if Dipple's sold any plant food that cost less than three dollars.

Thomas decided he'd go inside the store after Arthur came back. He looked at the clock outside the bank across the street. What was taking Arthur so long, anyway?

Then the automatic doors opened, and Arthur came out. He was carrying a bulging paper bag.

"You got the flowers, huh?" said Thomas.

"Sort of."

"What do you mean sort of?"

Arthur said, "They didn't have any daffodils growing in pots. And the saleswoman told me the bulbs have to be planted months ahead of time."

"Oh." Thomas eyed Arthur's paper bag. "So what did you do?"

"I bought these." Arthur reached into his bag and pulled out a bunch of blossoms.

Thomas thought they looked great. The leaves were a glossy green, and the petals were bright yellow.

Then he took a closer look. "Hey, Arthur, those flowers are made of plastic!"

Arthur nodded. "Yep. I'm gonna stick them in the ground, anyway. I figure it might be a whole week before Mom notices."

»6«

The Disturbance
at Dipple's

Thomas stared at Arthur. Substituting plastic daffodils for real ones seemed like a strange idea. But
who knew? It might work.

Anyway, now it was his turn to look around the
store. Thomas found the garden supply department
at the rear. After searching through dusty cans of
fertilizer, he picked out the smallest container.

But even that small one cost two dollars and
sixty-nine cents. And there would be sales tax, too.
Buying the plant food would take almost all of his
three dollars!

Oh, well, he thought, as he headed for the front

of the store. He did want Lucky to become a healthy bean plant.

As he passed through the music section, he saw a bearded man browsing among the compact discs. Besides snowy-white whiskers, the man had a large pot belly.

He reminded Thomas of someone. Santa Claus, that was who! But why was the fellow wearing such a long, heavy coat? It wasn't that cold outside. Thomas shrugged and moved on.

When he got outside, Arthur and Lizzie were both sitting on a bench near the door. "Did you buy anything?" asked Arthur.

Thomas nodded and took the can of plant food out of the bag to show them. "I had to spend almost all my money," he said in a resigned voice.

He admired the candy bars in a vending machine near the store's entrance, while Lizzie climbed into the wagon. Then the automatic door wheezed open. The man with the snowy-white beard was about to leave the store.

Lizzie stood still and stared. "Is that Santa Claus?" she whispered.

The security guard was following right behind him. The bearded man glanced over his shoulder. Then—suddenly!—he began to run. The guard lunged at him, making a grab for the man's long coat and missing it.

Thomas watched with amazement as they raced by him. Why was the bearded man running? And why was the guard dashing after him?

Lizzie cried, "That mean man is chasing Santa Claus!"

The bearded man swerved to avoid the wagon, almost sideswiping Arthur. He zigged and zagged, ran around a lamp post, and then doubled back again.

"What's going on?" Thomas called to Arthur.

"I dunno." Arthur pointed to the bearded man. "But he's pretty fast for a big guy."

The security guard was just a few steps behind the other fellow when the guard skidded on the sidewalk. He lost his balance, and the bearded man shot forward.

The man headed for the narrow space between Thomas and the building. Thomas jumped to get out of his way, but the bearded man suddenly changed direction. Too late, Thomas saw what was happening. He couldn't stop.

Thunk! They bumped right into each other.

"Umpf!" The bearded man grunted as he went sprawling onto the sidewalk.

Thomas felt as if he'd been whacked by a three-hundred pound pillow. He staggered, then tumbled on top of the man.

"Ooooh!" the man groaned.

Thomas felt dazed. The security guard helped him up. Then the guard pulled out a set of handcuffs and fastened the bearded man's hands behind his back!

The guard reached into the man's coat pockets and pulled out several compact discs. He spoke into his walkie-talkie, and another uniformed fellow came out of the building.

"Please don't leave yet," the security guard said to Thomas. "I'll be right back." Then the two guards led the bearded man back into the store.

"I bet that bearded guy was a criminal," Thomas said.

"Yeah!" said Arthur.

When the guard returned in a few minutes, he said, "It's a good thing you stopped that guy. He was shoplifting."

"I thought so," Thomas said.

"If I'd known that in the beginning," said Arthur, "I would have jumped on him, too."

But Lizzie was angry. She marched up to the security guard and said, "What did you do to Santa Claus?"

"Uh . . . nothing," said the guard.

"He's not really Santa Claus," Arthur told Lizzie.

"Oh." Lizzie looked relieved.

"I'm going to find the owners of the store," the guard said to Thomas. "I'm sure they'll want to express their gratitude."

"What did he say they were gonna press?" Arthur asked as soon as the guard went back inside.

Thomas shrugged. "Beats me. I don't know why he wants us to hang around."

Two men wearing business suits came out of

the building. The taller one looked at Thomas. "Are you the young man who captured the shoplifter?"

Thomas stared at him. "Well . . ." He glanced at Arthur, who was nodding his head rapidly. "I guess so. But I didn't really—"

Arthur said, "He's the one, all right!"

"Good," said the tall man. "I am Edward Dipple, and this is my brother, Frank."

"Uh, hello," said Thomas. "This is my friend Arthur." He didn't introduce Lizzie because he didn't trust her to behave herself.

Arthur held out his hand to Mr. Edward Dipple. "I have a goldfish named Ed," he said.

Mr. Dipple raised his eyebrows. "How . . . nice." Then he turned to Thomas. "Ahem. We wish to give you a small token of our appreciation."

Frank smiled. "You can pick out anything in the store you want—"

"Under ten dollars," Edward Dipple added hastily.

"Wow!" said Arthur.

Thomas grinned. Everyone, including Lizzie,

went back inside Dipple's Dime Store.

Let's see, thought Thomas, as he looked around. I'll start with a couple of comic books, then maybe eight or ten packs of gum . . .

As he wondered what else to choose, a tiny paperback book in a display near the check-out counter caught his eye. Leafing through it, he discovered that he could read most of the words. He studied the cover.

How to Get Better Grades
DO WELL IN SCHOOL
WITHOUT EVEN TRYING!

Thomas thought he would like to get better grades—especially if he didn't have to work hard. And the book only cost eighty-nine cents.

"I'll take this, too," he said, holding up the little book.

Then he noticed a new type of toy car that he'd seen advertised on television. "And that!" he said, pointing.

"Thanks a lot," Thomas said to the Dipples as the cashier put his selections into a paper bag.

The Dipple brothers smiled at him. "Thank

you!" they both said at once. Thomas and Arthur said goodbye to the security guard, too, and even Lizzie waved to him as they left.

They went back to Arthur's house afterwards to play with Thomas's new car. By the time Thomas finally got home, Mr. and Mrs. Tuttle had already started dinner.

"Wait till you hear what happened," Thomas said, as he slid into his chair. He told his parents about the shoplifter.

"I tried to get out of his way, but I ended up crashing into him," he said. "And the funny thing was that the people at the store treated me like a hero."

Mrs. Tuttle almost dropped the bowl of mashed potatoes. "Why, you could've gotten hurt!" she said.

Thomas wrinkled his forehead in thought. "I don't think so, Mom," he said at last, "unless that guy had fallen on me, instead of the other way around."

He began shaping his potatoes into a volcano. He made a crater in the top. Then he filled it with margarine lava.

Mr. Tuttle whistled and shook his head. "The shoplifter might have escaped if you hadn't been there," he said. That made Thomas feel pretty good—even if he wasn't a hero on purpose.

After dinner, he went to the garage and mixed up a little of the plant food with water. He took the mixture up to his room and carefully poured it over his bean plant.

He was hoping that right away the stem would stand up straight and tall and the leaves would instantly plump out. That didn't happen, but he thought Lucky looked a bit less droopy.

"Are you feeling better, little guy?" he said. Then he glanced over his shoulder to make sure nobody had heard him.

"Don't worry," he whispered, "you'll be big and strong in no time."

»7«

Another Project!

Things were looking up, Thomas decided, as he got ready for school on Monday morning. He had foiled a shoplifter. His bean plant was probably getting healthier. And one of these days, he'd get around to reading that book, *How to Get Better Grades*.

But the first thing Mrs. Findlay did was to spoil his happy mood. She assigned another project.

"Next Monday, March twenty-fifth, is Maryland Day," she said. "To celebrate, I want each of you to do a short report."

Oh boy, thought Thomas. That's not what I call a celebration.

"The reports will be about important people from Maryland history," said Mrs. Findlay. "I'll give you an example. Has anyone in the class visited Fort McHenry National Park?"

"Me! Me!" Beverly Ann waved her arm in the air.

Thomas raised his hand, too. He and his parents had visited the fort just two weeks ago.

Mrs. Findlay beamed. "I'm sure both of you can name an important historical figure who's associated with the fort. How about you, Thomas?"

"Uh . . ." Thomas knew that British ships had attacked the fort. And some man had written "The Star-Spangled Banner" when he saw the flag still waving after the battle. What was that fellow's name?

Beverly Ann said, "It's—"

"I asked Thomas, Beverly Ann." Mrs. Findlay frowned at her. "Please let him answer."

Thomas stared down at his desk. If only he could remember! He thought the name had something to do with a doorway. No, not a doorway . . .

a lock. Yeah! "Francis Scott Key," Thomas said triumphantly.

"Very good," said Mrs. Findlay. Then she turned to the whole class. "If the British troops had won that battle in 1814, they might have gone on and taken over Baltimore."

Mary Lynne said, "Would that make us part of England?"

Arthur said, "I wouldn't like being part of England. We'd have to drink a whole lot of tea." He made a face. "Ugh!"

Everybody started talking at once. "Tea? Blah!"

"Not me!"

"No way!"

Mrs. Findlay clapped her hands. "One person at a time, please."

She pointed to Charlie Rivera, who'd been patiently waiting with his hand raised. "Charlie, do you have something to say?"

"Yes," he said, in a troubled voice. "I can't drink a lot of tea, Mrs. Findlay. Last time I had the flu, my mother made me swallow a whole cupful, and then I threw up!"

"Oh," said Mrs. Findlay. "I'm sorry to hear that." Then she called on Chelsea.

"Iced tea with lemon is good," Chelsea said. "Why don't we have that instead of hot tea?"

"Yeah!" said Mary Lynne in a loud whisper.

Abigail said, "Let's take a vote!"

"Iced tea is very refreshing," agreed Mrs. Findlay. She glanced at her watch. "But now, we need to talk some more about Maryland Day—"

Arthur's hand was high in the air. With one knee on his chair, he was halfway out of his seat.

Mrs. Findlay sighed. "Is it important, Arthur?"

"Yeah!" Arthur jumped to his feet. "No matter what those girls say"—he glanced at Chelsea, Mary Lynne, and Abigail—"I don't think we should have any tea at all."

Mrs. Findlay shook her head. "I don't want to hear another word about tea!"

Thomas leaned way over and yanked at Arthur's jeans. "Sit down!" he hissed. "The teacher's getting mad at you!"

Arthur sank down in his chair. But now Charlie

had his hand up again.

"Yes, Charlie," said Mrs. Findlay. "What is it?"

"What about those funny English accents? Do we have to talk like that, too?"

Mrs. Findlay sighed. "No, Charlie. We won the War of 1812. This is the United States of America, remember?"

She tapped her pencil on her open palm while she glanced around the room. Gradually, the third graders became very quiet.

"All right," Mrs. Findlay said. "I want to explain exactly what you should do for your reports."

The teacher cleared her throat. "Come to school on Monday dressed as a famous person from Maryland history. And be prepared to tell us something about him or her."

Chelsea said she didn't think her mother would have time to sew a costume. But Mrs. Findlay said the outfits didn't have to be fancy.

"Just look around your house and see what you can find," she said. "And remember to tell me ahead of time whom your report is about, so I can make sure that they're all different."

She told the class to get out their spelling workbooks. "Oh, and there's one more thing about the reports—I'm going to give prizes for the best ones!"

When the class went outside for morning recess, everyone was talking about Maryland Day. "I know what I'm doing," Arthur said, "a report on dinosaurs."

Thomas stared at him in surprise. But Charlie said, "Wow! What a great idea!"

"Ye-ah," Thomas said slowly, "but I'm not sure Mrs. Findlay will like it."

"Of course not!" snapped Beverly Ann. "It's totally dumb."

Arthur crossed his arms on his chest. "Oh, yeah? Dinosaurs lived millions of years ago. Now they're gone. They're history, all right."

Thomas still wasn't sure. "But are any of them famous? And did any come from Maryland?"

Arthur had a stubborn look on his face. "I don't know. But I'm going to find out."

Beverly Ann rolled her eyes, but Arthur

ignored her. "What about you?" he asked Thomas. "Who are you going to do your report on?"

"I'm not sure," Thomas said. He thought a minute. "I know. I'll be Francis Scott Key. I got a pamphlet at Fort McHenry that tells all about him."

Beverly Ann leaned forward, her hands on her hips. "Hey! *I'm* going to be Francis Scott Key!"

"I said it first!" Thomas said.

He thought of the three-cornered hat his parents had bought him on their trip to Williamsburg, Virginia. "I even have something to wear."

"I don't care. I should be Francis Scott Key because I'm a better singer than you are."

"Huh? What's singing got to do with it?"

"Francis Scott Key wrote 'The Star-Spangled Banner,' so I'm planning to sing it for my report."

"Oh, no!" Arthur smacked his forehead with the heel of his hand. "You mean we have to listen to you holler?"

"No," said Thomas, "because she's not doing Francis Scott Key. I am."

Beverly Ann said, "You'll just mess it up."

"I will not!" said Thomas angrily. "I bet I'll even win a prize!"

"Huh! I've never heard of you winning any prizes!" Beverly Ann said, and she flounced off.

Arthur stared at Thomas. "Why did you say you were going to win? Your projects are always the worst in the class."

"I know," said Thomas. "But this one is going to be different. This time I'm going to get a good grade."

"How come?"

"Because I'm going to go home after school and get out that little book I got at Dipple's Dime Store. After that, no problem!"

»8«

Gobbledegook

"**T**hose girls are talking about you," Arthur said at recess the next day. He pointed to a group of third graders standing around the tire swing.

"How do you know?" asked Thomas. He peered at the girls over Arthur's shoulder.

"Easy," Arthur said. "Beverly Ann's pointing at you. And they're all looking this way."

"Well, maybe they're looking at *you*."

Arthur shrugged. "I don't think so. See, I'll go over here." He ducked behind a tree. "They're still looking your way."

Thomas didn't want anybody looking at him. "Yeah," he said unhappily. "I guess you're right."

Arthur walked back. "Hey!" he said as he dug his elbow into Thomas's ribs. "They're coming over here!"

Thomas looked across the playground. Marching toward them was the entire group of girls—Beverly Ann, Lucy Burnett, Katie Klein, Abigail MacCready, Chelsea Martin, and Mary Lynne Woodlie.

Beverly Ann stopped in front of Thomas. With her feet spread wide apart and her arms crossed, she looked as if she meant business.

"I told them what you said yesterday." Beverly Ann pointed toward the other girls. "And they don't believe me. So, you tell them."

"Tell them what?" Thomas asked.

"Tell them that what I said you said is true."

"Tell them what I said you said? But I don't remember what you said."

"No, no." Beverly Ann shook her head in a disgusted way. "Not what you said I said. What I said you said!"

Huh? Thomas looked at Arthur. Arthur was drawing circles in the air next to his ear.

Beverly Ann frowned at Arthur. "Oh, don't be so silly!"

"Me?" Arthur raised his eyebrows and jerked his thumb toward his chest. "Silly? I'm not silly, and neither is Thomas."

"Yeah," Thomas said. "You're the one who's talking gobbledegook!"

Beverly Ann stamped her foot. "I'm not talking gobbledegook!"

The other girls giggled. Mary Lynne said, "We're talking about the Maryland Day reports."

Chelsea nodded. "She told us you think you're going to do the best report in the class."

"Oh!" Thomas was embarrassed. "I didn't say that exactly—"

"Yes, you did." Beverly Ann waggled her finger back and forth in front of Thomas's nose.

Thomas felt his eyes crossing as he tried to follow the movement. "I meant I'm going to try to win a prize."

Beverly Ann turned to the other girls. "See? He *did* say it. I told you so!"

She turned back to Thomas. "You can just forget

about that. *I'm* going to win, and you're not."

"Oh, yeah?" Thomas and Arthur both spoke at once.

"Yeah!"

Thweet! *Thweet*! *Thweet*! Mrs. Findlay stood at the other end of the playground, blowing her whistle. It was the signal that recess was over.

As the girls scattered, Thomas and Arthur headed for the side door. "At least you don't have to worry about your report," said Arthur.

Thomas looked at him. "Why not?"

"You've got that book—*How To Get Better Grades*. You probably know all the secrets by now, right?"

"Well," said Thomas, "not exactly."

"What do you mean? I thought you were going to look at the book yesterday after school."

"Yeah, but . . . I never got around to it."

"Oh, boy!" Arthur said. "You're hopeless. I'm going home with you today and make you read it."

"All right," said Thomas. It wasn't going to be any big deal. The book cover said you could get better grades without even trying.

When they arrived at Thomas's house after school, they got something to eat and then went up to his bedroom. At first, Thomas couldn't find the book. He searched for five minutes and then discovered it under a dirty plate on his desk.

"Okay," said Arthur, flopping down on Thomas's bed. "Go ahead. Read."

Thomas groaned. This wasn't the kind of book he liked. Even though he was the one who'd picked it out, he hadn't thought he'd actually have to *read* it. He'd imagined that somehow just owning it would help.

With a sigh, he sat down in his desk chair. He opened the book to page one.

Arthur started humming a song the third grade had learned in music class that day. Then he leaned over and took some rubber bands from Thomas's desk. He started snapping them at the ceiling.

"Hah!" said Thomas suddenly. He threw the book across the room.

Arthur sat up straight. "What's wrong?"

"They lied!" said Thomas. "That book says you

have to write down your assignments and read over your notes—a bunch of stuff like that. So, you *do* have to try! I'm not reading it anymore."

Arthur said, "I always write down the assignments. How else are you gonna know what to do?"

Thomas shrugged. "I just try to remember them."

Arthur gave Thomas a questioning look. "Are you going to give up?"

Thomas thought a minute. He wanted to end up with a good report, didn't he? "No, I'm not gonna give up," he said with a sigh. He plodded across the room and picked up the book.

Bothersome Beeping

Thomas sprawled on the floor, his eyes fastened on the television screen. Without looking, he reached out and grabbed a handful of microwave popcorn from a paper bag.

Crunch . . . crunch . . . beep!

Beep? What was that?

Beep-a-beep-beep-beep! The noise was getting louder. *Beep-beep-a-beep*!

Thomas tore his gaze away from the television screen. Where was that annoying sound coming from?

Then he remembered. It was the timer that he'd brought out from the kitchen.

The beeping meant he was supposed to stop watching cartoons. He needed to work on his Francis Scott Key report.

I'll just watch another five minutes of TV, Thomas told himself. But just then, he heard a different sound. *Brrinng! Brrinng! Brrinng!*

Hey!—what was that?

Thomas looked around the room. Oh, yeah— the radio alarm clock. He'd carried it down from his parents' room and plugged it into an outlet in the living room.

He looked at the clock in disgust. Okay, okay, he told himself, I give up! He pressed the small black button which stopped the alarm. Sighing, he trudged up to his room.

According to the little paperback book, he was supposed to break up a task into small steps. So, he was trying to write his report a little at a time.

He had one, two, three . . . ten words on an index card. He thought he'd better write a bit more than that.

He sat down at his desk and studied the Fort McHenry pamphlet. I'll work for fifteen minutes, he decided, and then watch the rest of that TV show. He got the timer from downstairs and set it.

When the alarm went off, Thomas put down his pencil and looked over his index cards. He'd gotten a lot done in those fifteen minutes—thirty more words.

He figured he was about halfway through the report. He deserved a break now. But he thought he'd better set the alarm again and carry the timer with him.

The next time he heard the beeping sound, Thomas found it easier to get back to work on the report. Just a little more writing, he promised himself, and then he'd be finished.

Ten minutes later, Thomas set his paper and pencil aside. He stood and stretched. His report was done! He'd finished even before the alarm went off, and he felt really good.

Then he heard the telephone ringing. It's probably Arthur, he thought, as he picked up the receiver. "Hello?"

Giggle . . . giggle . . . giggle!

Huh? That didn't sound like Arthur. Thomas

took the phone away from his ear and gave it a shake.

"Hello?" he said again.

Giggle . . . *snort* . . . giggle! Then Thomas heard Mary Lynne's voice. "Sorry," she said. "Chelsea said something funny just as you picked up the phone."

"Oh," Thomas said in a grumpy voice. He couldn't help wondering if Chelsea was making a joke about him.

"Well, what do you want?"

"We're just calling to find out if you've started working on your report yet," Mary Lynne said. "The Maryland Day project is due on Monday, you know."

"Don't worry," Thomas said proudly. "My report is all done."

"Really?"

Thomas could hear the low murmur of voices. Then Mary Lynne was back on the line. "Chelsea wants to know if you have your costume ready."

Costume? Thomas felt like a balloon that had just been pricked by a sharp pin. "Well, no-o-o," he admitted. "I sort of forgot about that."

"You mean, you haven't even thought about what you're going to wear?" Mary Lynne sounded anxious.

"Uh . . . not much."

"Don't you think you'd better—"

"Yes," Thomas said. "I will."

"But—wait a minute," said Mary Lynne. Thomas heard Chelsea speaking in the background. "Chelsea says maybe we'd better come over and help you find a costume."

"No, you don't have to do that!" Thomas was feeling very suspicious. "Why are you so interested, anyway?"

"We made a bet with Beverly Ann. She said you wouldn't even get a report done by Monday, and we said you would."

"Oh," Thomas said. "Well, you don't have to worry."

"That's good. See ya!"

"Goodbye!" said Thomas. He hung up the phone.

Hmmm. He had that three-cornered hat. But

what else could he wear to look like Francis Scott Key?

Thomas took out his Fort McHenry pamphlet and looked at the picture of Key, dressed in his old-fashioned clothes. Then he tapped nervously on his front teeth. He had a few ideas, but maybe he'd better call Arthur.

Arthur had said he didn't have to worry about his own costume; his mother was sewing it for him. But he might be able to come up with some suggestions for Thomas's outfit. Thomas figured he needed all the help he could get.

»10«

Mrs. Wilmot's Wig

"**W**hat're those blue squiggles all over your hand?" Arthur asked. He and Thomas were up in Arthur's bedroom.

"Those aren't squiggles," said Thomas. "Those are words. I decided what I needed to find for my costume, and I wrote it down."

"Oh," said Arthur. "I write stuff down, too, but I put it on paper."

Thomas was a little embarrassed. "I tried that," he said, "but then I kept forgetting to look at the paper."

Arthur had been unraveling the core of a golf ball that his father had accidentally split open with the lawn mower. It was full of tightly wrapped elastic string.

He put down the ball. "Let me see."

He grabbed Thomas's hand and pulled it under his nose. "Hmmm . . . the ink's kind of blurry."

"That's because I washed my hands."

Arthur said, "I don't understand. What does this"—he poked his finger at the words—"have to do with finding a Francis Scott Key outfit?"

"What do you mean?"

"Well, you wrote 'Mind a pig.' Or is it, 'Climb a fig'?"

Thomas rolled his eyes. "No! It says, 'Find a wig.' Two hundred years ago, men wore wigs on top of their hair."

"Yeah, I know," said Arthur. "I always wondered why."

Thomas shrugged. "Maybe they didn't want to worry about keeping their hair combed."

Arthur picked up the golf ball again. He pulled out the end of the elastic and started winding it around a pencil. "My mom has a wig. D'you want to see it?"

"I guess so," said Thomas.

Arthur went to find the wig. When he came back, he was carrying a deep, round cardboard box. He lifted up the lid. "Ta-da!"

Thomas stared into the box. Perched on an egg-shaped piece of styrofoam was a mop of curly blonde hair.

He shook his head. "I don't think that's the right kind of wig."

"Why not?" Arthur took the wig out of the box. "Here, try it on," he said and jammed the wig down on Thomas's head.

"It needs to be pulled back into one of those little ponytails," said Arthur. "Just wait a minute, you'll see."

He found a rubber band and fiddled with it behind Thomas's back.

Thomas was getting impatient. The wig was making him hot, and it pushed down his ears uncomfortably.

"Okay," said Arthur. "All done."

"Let me see." Thomas moved over to the mirror that hung above Arthur's dresser.

"Aaaah!" He stared at his reflection.

Long yellow curls tumbled over his forehead, and corkscrew ringlets drooped down on one shoulder. Thomas thought this was the way Goldilocks must have looked after she'd been frightened by the bears.

"Hmmm," Arthur said. "Now that I get a better look at you, I think it's a good thing you're not a girl."

"Thanks!" muttered Thomas. He yanked off the wig and tossed it to Arthur.

Arthur shrugged. "I was just trying to help."

"I know. Does your mom have any other wigs?"

"Well . . . maybe in the attic."

Thomas had seen the Wilmots' big, old-fashioned attic once a long time ago, and he longed to explore it more thoroughly. "Can we go up and look?"

"Yeah, as long as Mom doesn't find out. She doesn't like me to go in the attic."

"Why?" Thomas asked.

"She says I might get hurt somehow. But

there's just a lot of old junk up there."

Arthur went over to the window and looked down. "Oh, that's good," he said. "She's still working on the flowerbed."

Thomas went to the window, too. He could hardly believe what he saw. In the yard below was Mrs. Wilmot, with Lizzie beside her, pulling weeds from the bed of plastic daffodils.

"Hey," he said, "doesn't your mom know those are fake flowers?"

"Oh, yeah. She caught on right away." Arthur looked sheepish. "At first she was mad. But then she told me she was gonna leave the flowers there for awhile. She said at least she didn't have to worry about them wilting."

Arthur stuck the golf ball and pencil in his pocket. "Come on, let's go up in the attic now while Mom's still outside."

He led the way to a deep hallway closet. Inside, behind a rack of coats, a stairway rose steeply to a trapdoor.

Arthur scrambled to the top. He unfastened a wooden latch and pushed up the trapdoor.

Thomas tilted his head back to look up. Beyond the square opening was a huge, dark space.

"Wow!" he said. "I didn't remember that your attic was this big."

"Turn on the light," said Arthur, pointing to a switch on the closet wall.

When Thomas turned the light on, the space above got a little brighter. But not much.

"Come on up," said Arthur. Then he disappeared through the opening.

Thomas started up the stairs. There was no telling what they'd find. There could be practically anything up there.

Thump, Thump!

Thomas stepped gingerly up into the attic. The edges of the room were shadowy. One bare bulb hung on a cord from the middle of the ceiling.

The floorboards looked worn and much older than he remembered. He hoped they were good and sturdy and not full of wood-eating bugs.

But what if the boards *were* full of bugs—termites, for example? And what if he stepped on a weak spot, where the insects had already chewed through the wood?

Thomas imagined his legs crashing through the attic floor. I'd still be okay, he thought. I'd throw out my arms to catch myself.

But what if the hole was wider than his arms could reach? Then his entire body would go hurtling into the space below!

And where would he end up? What room was below this part of the attic? Thomas tried to picture the second level of Arthur's house. He was standing above the bathroom.

Uh-oh. What if he broke through the floor exactly over the toilet? And what if the lid was up? Oh, no! Thomas closed his eyes briefly. He could just see himself landing—splash!—right in the toilet bowl.

"Hey, Arthur," he said. "Have your parents ever had an exterminator come to check out this place?"

Arthur looked surprised. "I don't think so. Why?"

"Just wondering," said Thomas. But when Arthur walked farther into the attic, Thomas stayed close behind him.

Arthur took two steps, and the boards beneath his feet went *cr-r-eak.* Then Thomas took a step. *Cr-r-eak* went the floor.

Suddenly Arthur whirled around. "Why are you following me?"

Thomas just shrugged. He looked around at the attic crammed with stuff. The floor hadn't collapsed yet. If Arthur wasn't worried, maybe he shouldn't be either.

Thomas started to explore on his own. He took a few steps and then froze. Not far away, a furry gray animal crouched on top of a chest of drawers. The creature had huge teeth and glittering eyes. Thomas shuddered. This must be the largest rat in the world!

Then he noticed the broad tail and moth-eaten fur. He stepped closer. This wasn't a rat. And it wasn't alive!

"Hey, Arthur!" he called. "What's this?"

Arthur came and stood beside him. "Oh, that's a beaver. Isn't he great? He died a few years ago, and my uncle Harold stuffed him."

Thomas looked around to see what else was in the attic. On either end of the long room were little square windows that looked as if they hadn't been washed for twenty years. Raindrops began to spatter against the panes. There was a far-off sound of thunder, and Thomas realized the room was starting to get even darker.

"We'd better hurry," said Arthur. He pointed to a big black trunk. "There might be a wig in there."

"All right." Thomas started picking his way across the floor.

All of a sudden, a spider dropped down in front of his face. For a moment, it dangled there, swinging to and fro.

Thomas wasn't afraid of spiders. But this one looked big enough to make a galloping sound when it ran.

He stumbled backwards. An old shovel with a broken handle was lying in wait. He stepped on the shovel, and his foot went sideways, twisting his ankle.

"Oooh! Aaah!" Thomas grabbed his ankle and hopped up and down.

Arthur frowned. "Hey, don't make so much noise. Mom probably came inside when it started raining. She might hear us."

"I couldn't help it." Thomas pointed to the

shovel. "That thing tripped me."

"Come on." Arthur was kneeling in front of the trunk. Thomas joined him, and together they pushed up the heavy lid.

A peculiar odor rushed out. Thomas thought it was that same smell that came from the closet at home—mothballs.

He looked inside the trunk and picked up the first thing he saw—a pancake-shaped object made of soft, black cloth. "Hey, look—a velvet Frisbee."

Arthur shook his head. "I think that's a hat."

Thomas was reaching into the trunk again when he heard a noise. *Thump!* There was a short pause, then another *thump!*

"What's that?"

Arthur's eyes opened wide. "It sounds like footsteps. Somebody's coming up the stairs."

Thump! . . . *thump!* . . . *thump!*

"Is it your mom?" whispered Thomas.

"I don't think so. Her feet aren't that big."

If it wasn't Mrs. Wilmot, who could it be? The skin on the back of Thomas's neck felt prickly.

"Who do you s'pose it is?" he whispered to Arthur.

Arthur's eyes became even rounder. "I don't know. What do you think?"

Images flashed one after another through Thomas's mind. He thought of a vampire, curling back its lips in a horrifying smile . . . a mummy, dragging tattered wrappings as it limped along . . . or even Frankenstein's monster, its powerful arms dangling as it lurched up the attic stairs.

Thomas swallowed. "It could be anybody."

In the dim light, he stared at the trapdoor opening. He held his breath, and a moment later saw two little hands grip the edge. Then Lizzie's head popped into view.

Thomas let out his breath, and frowned. Dumb old Lizzie!

"What are you doing here?" said Arthur. "How'd you find us?"

Lizzie reached down to pick up a shoebox from the step below, then came up into the attic. "I saw you go into the closet. I want to show you my new pet."

She clumped toward them, and Thomas saw that she was wearing a pair of rubber boots that were several sizes too big. So that was what had made all the noise.

After taking off the lid, she held out the shoe-box so the boys could look inside.

The box was filled with grass, leaves, and a few twigs. That was all, as far as Thomas could see.

"What are you talking about?" Arthur said. "There's nothing in there."

Lizzie started poking in the grass. "I think he's hiding."

She squatted on the floor and pulled out some of the leaves. She picked them up one by one, examining both sides. Finally, she turned the shoe-box upside down and shook it. The rest of the grass and twigs fell onto the floor.

"Where are you, Antie?" she said.

A tiny brown ant ran out from under a leaf and scurried across the floor. A few seconds later, it had disappeared into a crack between two boards.

Thomas whispered to Arthur, "Her new pet is an ant?"

Arthur shrugged. "I guess so."

Lizzie got on her hands and knees and put her face close to the crack. "Come back here, Antie!"

After a minute, she got to her feet. "He's gone," she said. There were tears in her eyes.

Arthur looked at Thomas. "If she starts bawling," he said, "Mom will come to see what's wrong. And then we'll be in trouble!"

Uh-oh, thought Thomas. "Don't worry," he told Lizzie quickly. "We'll find you a new ant."

"You will?" said Lizzie. "Right now?"

"Sure," said Arthur. "When it stops raining."

Lizzie pointed to the window. "It already did stop."

Arthur sighed. "Oh, all right. We'll do it now."

He started for the stairway. "Wait a minute. We didn't find your wig yet."

"That's all right," Thomas said. "Maybe my mom knows someone who owns a wig." He thought he would just as soon get out of the attic before Arthur's mother discovered them.

"But what are you going to do about a costume?" Arthur said.

Thomas shrugged. "I don't know. I wish I

could find something that looks old-fashioned. Like a uniform, maybe."

Then Lizzie piped up. "I know where to find a uniform!"

Thomas stared at her. "You do?"

"Don't pay any attention to her," Arthur scoffed.

Lizzie glared at her brother. "I do, too, know where a uniform is."

She turned and pointed to a far corner of the attic. Thomas could just make out a dim shape hanging from a rickety hall tree. "It's right over there."

"Hey, she's right!" said Arthur after the two boys went to investigate. "It looks like the jacket my big brother wore in the marching band."

"It's perfect," Thomas said in an excited voice. He held up the navy blue garment and admired the gold braid and shiny brass buttons.

Thomas slipped the jacket over his shoulders. "Do you think Jason would mind if I borrowed it?"

"Naw," said Arthur. "He won't mind."

Arthur and Lizzie started down the attic stairs

with Thomas following right behind. Thomas could hardly believe his good luck.

By the time he got home, he had the rest of his outfit all figured out. Instead of wearing a wig, he could shake talcum powder on his hair to make it white.

Now all he needed to do was find some knee socks. This is going to be a great costume, Thomas told himself. Beverly Ann had better watch out!

»12«

An Unpleasant Surprise

On Monday morning, Thomas got dressed in his Francis Scott Key outfit. Hmmm, not bad, he thought, as he looked into the long hallway mirror.

He flicked a bit of lint off his jacket. It was roomy; he had to roll up the sleeves. But the brass buttons were so shiny that when he looked down he could see his face in them.

He touched his powdered hair, and a cloud of white particles flew into the air. He sneezed— "Aachoo!"

Then he gave a tug to his mother's white knee socks. He pulled them up until they reached his pants, which he'd rolled up to his knees. He gently set his three-cornered black hat on his head and decided he was ready.

But he needed to give some water to Lucky. "Hey, Lucky," he said, "I can't believe it. You're getting a new leaf!"

His Maryland Day report was done, and his bean plant was definitely growing. Nothing could go wrong now.

The doorbell rang, and a moment later his mother called to him. "Thomas, are you ready? Arthur's here!"

Thomas had been wondering whether Arthur would actually go through with his idea of giving a dinosaur report. And now he knew. From his headpiece all the way to his feet, Arthur was covered in mottled gray-brown cloth.

"You look great!" Thomas said.

Arthur grinned. "Thanks." He swiveled so that Thomas could see his long tail.

Thomas said, "I like the color. It looks like a real dinosaur."

Arthur nodded. "Yeah, I think dinosaurs probably had the same sort of skin as elephants."

"Or rhinoceroses."

"Or hippopotamuses," said Arthur. He looked at Thomas. "Your outfit's good, too."

"Uh-huh." Thomas was proud of his costume, and he couldn't wait to show it off.

"What do you think Mrs. Findlay will say about your report?" Thomas asked as they walked to school.

"I'm not worried," Arthur said. "She'll like it."

Thomas wasn't so sure. But at least he didn't have to worry about his project. This time, he told himself happily, Mrs. Findlay would have nothing but nice things to say to him.

Soon he and Arthur came to the intersection that was a block from school. Waiting at the crosswalk was Charlie Rivera. He was dressed in a baseball uniform and was carrying a bat and glove.

"Who are you?" Thomas asked as they crossed the street.

"I'm Babe Ruth," Charlie said.

The crossing guard stopped the traffic again, and a group of children came walking across the street. Beverly Ann was in front. When she caught sight of Arthur, she stopped suddenly, and a first grader ran into her from behind.

"I can't believe you really did your report on a dinosaur," Beverly Ann said. "You're going to get in trouble!"

Arthur scowled. "I am not!"

"Yes, you are!"

Thomas was only half-listening to the argument. He was busy studying Beverly Ann's costume.

Her hair was covered by a gray wig, tied at the back of her neck with a black bow. Her shirt was white with lace at the collar and cuffs. Over it, she wore a man's suit vest. Like Thomas, she wore knee socks and pants rolled up to her knees.

Thomas had an uneasy feeling. "Who are you supposed to be?" he said.

Beverly Ann tossed her head. "Francis Scott Key, of course."

Thomas said, "But, *I'm* Francis Scott Key."

Beverly Ann raised her eyebrows. "No, I am."

Arthur scowled, and Charlie looked worried. "You can't both be him," Charlie said.

"Mrs. Findlay said all the reports have to be different."

"I know that," Beverly Ann said smugly. "I went to her the day she announced the project and told her I was doing my report on Francis Scott Key."

Thomas gaped at her. "You did?"

Beverly Ann nodded. "She wrote it in her book."

Thomas stared down at a crack in the sidewalk. He remembered Mrs. Findlay reminding the class to check with her about the report topics.

So he'd messed up again. He'd forgotten to check with Mrs. Findlay about his subject. But Beverly Ann hadn't forgotten.

Beverly Ann patted her wig. "I told Thomas I should be the one to do Francis Scott Key. I'm a better singer than he is."

"It still isn't fair," said Arthur.

"Too bad. The early bird gets the bug. He can do his report on someone else."

"Oh, sure!" Thomas said. Beverly Ann knew there wasn't time now for him to do a different report.

Charlie said, "Maybe you could talk to Mrs. Findlay. Maybe she'll let both of you do your reports on Francis Scott Key."

Thomas gave a tiny shrug. He felt hopeless; he let his shoulders sag. His knee socks were sagging, too, bagging around his ankles. He didn't bother to pull them up.

"He could ask Mrs. Findlay, at least." Arthur turned to Thomas. "What do you think?"

Thomas tried to imagine what would happen, and a picture of his teacher flashed into his mind. She was frowning. "You've done it again!" she was saying scornfully.

Thomas felt cold and clammy all over. "I think," he said, "I think . . . I'm going to be sick."

»13«

Thomas Has An Idea

"**H**ey, what's going on?" called Mary Lynne. She and Chelsea had just turned the corner. Both girls were wearing long skirts, and Chelsea had a ruffled cap on her head.

"Oh, nothing," Arthur answered. "Beverly Ann just stole Thomas's idea for Maryland Day, that's all."

"I did not!" Beverly Ann said indignantly. Her wig slipped sideways as she shook her head.

"Did, too! Thomas thought of it first."

"But he didn't tell Mrs. Findlay. And *I* did," Beverly Ann said, and she stalked off.

"Now," said Mary Lynne, "we'll lose our bet."

"Not if he does a report on somebody else," Chelsea pointed out.

"But he doesn't know anything about anybody else."

"Wait a minute," said Thomas. He was beginning to get an idea. He didn't know anything about another historical person. But he did know a lot about a historical *place.*

Thomas wasn't sure if his idea would work, but he thought he'd give it a try. "Go on ahead to school," he told Arthur. "I've got to go back home and get something."

Arthur raised his eyebrows. "You're going to be really late!" he warned.

"I don't care," Thomas said.

He turned the corner and headed home. When he got there, he let himself into the empty house.

As he ran upstairs, he struggled out of the navy blue jacket. While he unrolled his pants legs, he thought about the things he needed. Then he went down to the basement.

He spotted a big cardboard box and bumped it up the basement stairs. Then he found some masking tape and a couple of grocery sacks on a shelf in the garage.

Thomas cut open the bags and flattened them. After making a hole in the box, he taped the bags around the box to hide the letters printed on its sides. With an orange-red crayon, he drew on the brown paper. First he made a rectangle about six inches long and two inches wide. Then he colored it in.

He stood back and studied his work. Did the rectangle look like a brick? Yeah, especially if he squinted a little.

He went to work with his crayon. Soon he'd finished a line of bricks, like a train traveling across the paper. He did another row, and another.

Then he looked around the room. What else could he use for his costume?

The little cannons he'd bought at the Fort McHenry gift shop were guarding his dresser. They'd be perfect. Thomas used masking tape to fasten them to the top of the box, one on each side of the hole that he'd made for his head.

He glanced at the clock. He had to get going

now or he'd miss everything! With the big box in his arms, he hurried downstairs.

The sidewalks were empty of children, which made Thomas feel strange. He didn't like walking to school alone. After stopping at the office to pick up a late slip, he rushed down the empty hallway.

When he got to his classroom, Thomas opened the door a crack and looked in. Arthur was standing at the front of the room, and Mrs. Findlay was sitting at her desk.

Thomas tried to creep quietly into the room. Unfortunately, the door clicked when he shut it, and all the third graders swiveled their heads toward him. "You're late, Thomas," said Mrs. Findlay. "Do you have an excuse?"

"I have this paper." He held out the pink slip the office secretary had given him.

"All right," said Mrs. Findlay. Thomas put his box on the floor next to his chair and sat down.

Mrs. Findlay nodded to Arthur. "Go ahead with your report."

Arthur unfolded a sheet of paper. "My—"

Beverly Ann waved her arm back and forth.

Mrs. Findlay sighed. "What is it, Beverly Ann?"

"Are you really going to let Arthur give a report about dinosaurs?"

Quickly Arthur said, "My report isn't about just any old dinosaur. It's about a *Maryland* dinosaur."

Thomas smiled. He couldn't see Beverly Ann's face, but he heard her give a snort of disgust.

Mrs. Findlay looked at Arthur. "Go right ahead."

"My name is *Astrodon johnstoni*," Arthur said in a solemn voice. "I lived a hundred and thirty million years ago, and my bones have been found only in Maryland. I was taller than a small house and more than fifty feet long. I ate plants . . ."

When he finished, Mrs. Findlay said, "I'm curious, Arthur. Where did you get your information?"

"The story was in *The Sun* newspaper," Arthur said. "I found it in a pile in our basement."

"Good," said Mrs. Findlay. She asked who wanted to be next. Beverly Ann was the first to raise her hand.

"All right." Mrs. Findlay nodded at her.

When Beverly Ann got to the front of the room, she turned all around to show off her costume. Then she announced, "I am Francis Scott Key."

Thomas ground his teeth.

Beverly Ann stood with her hands clasped behind her back. "I was born in . . ."

Blah, blah, blah, thought Thomas. He didn't even want to listen.

"Next, I'm going to sing 'The Star-Spangled Banner,'" Beverly Ann said.

Thomas prepared himself to suffer.

»14«

Prizes

While Beverly Ann got out her copy of the anthem, Thomas decided to put on his costume. He turned his box upside down and grabbed the sides. Then he pulled it up and over his head.

But something was wrong. The bottom edge of the box touched the seat of his chair. That meant that its top was way above his head. He couldn't see a thing.

He scrambled onto his knees, popping his head through the opening. There, that was better.

"Stand up, everyone," said Mrs. Findlay.

Awkwardly, Thomas lurched to his feet. Inside the box, he put his right hand over his heart.

Beverly Ann bellowed, "O-h-h-h! say, can you see . . ."

She got to a high note, and Thomas winced. Over in the next row, Arthur stuck his fingers in his ears.

When she came to the end of the song, there were a few half-hearted claps. But most of the third graders sank into their seats with an air of relief.

Whew! thought Thomas. I'm glad that's over. He started to sit down. But again, the box got in his way.

Beverly Ann lingered at the front of the room. "Do you want to hear it again?"

"Oh!" Mrs. Findlay hesitated. "I'm not sure we have enough time."

"Don't worry," Beverly Ann assured her. "I can sing faster."

Arthur raised his hand. "Beverly Ann can't do an encore," he said. "We didn't clap enough."

"Oh, yeah?" Beverly Ann said. "Look at Thomas. He's standing up, and that shows he liked my performance. He wants me to sing."

Thomas was trying to take off the box. He'd managed to push it up a bit, but his head was still inside. "No, I don't!" he said in a muffled voice.

"What are you doing with that carton, Thomas?" said Mrs. Findlay.

Thomas let go of the box. It dropped to his shoulders, and his head popped out.

His face felt hot. It'd been stuffy inside there, and besides, he was flustered. "This is my costume. I can't sit down because it doesn't bend at the waist."

Mrs. Findlay raised her eyebrows. "I see. In that case, you'd better give your report next." She told Beverly Ann to sit down.

Nervously, Thomas went to stand by Mrs. Findlay's desk. He didn't have his report written out. What if he couldn't think of anything to say?

"First of all," said Mrs. Findlay, "I want to know who you're supposed to be. You never gave me the name of your famous Maryland person."

"I'm not a person," said Thomas. "I'm a thing. I'm Fort McHenry."

Mrs. Findlay glanced at the cannons that

Thomas had fastened to his carton. "All right. Go ahead."

For a second, Thomas's mind was blank. But then, suddenly, everything he knew about Fort McHenry came back to him. He took a deep breath and started. "Fort McHenry is right at the entrance to Baltimore Harbor . . . there's water on three sides . . ."

He looked at Mrs. Findlay and said, "It was built in the shape of a big star. But that was too complicated for me to make, so you'll have to imagine it."

"That's all right," said Mrs. Findlay. "Go on."

With long pauses, Thomas stumbled through his talk. He told about the battle in 1814 when the British bombarded the fort and about the huge guns that fired cannonballs back at them.

"If you visit the fort," he said, "you can go inside real barracks where soldiers used to live . . . and see the underground rooms where they kept the gunpowder."

When he couldn't think of any more facts, he said, "Uh . . . that's all."

Then Katie Klein raised her hand. "Why is your head white?"

Thomas had forgotten to brush the powder out of his hair! He thought fast. "That's snow. I'm Fort McHenry in winter."

"Okay," said Mrs. Findlay. Then she helped him take off his cardboard costume.

Thomas was glad *that* was over. He knew he hadn't given a great report. But maybe it was good enough to get a decent grade. At least Mrs. Findlay hadn't come right out and complained the way she had with the solar system project.

Now it was Chelsea Martin's turn. Carrying a threaded needle, a thimble, and some red and blue cloth, she walked to the front of the room.

"I am Mary Pickersgill," she said. "I made the large flag that flew over Fort McHenry when the British were bombarding it."

When she finished, Charlie put up his hand. "Why are you wearing that hat?"

Chelsea said, "Women wore caps like this in the early eighteen hundreds."

Then Arthur raised his hand. "My grandmother

crocheted one of those hats. She uses it in the bathroom to cover up a roll of toilet paper."

Mrs. Findlay frowned. "That's something entirely different, Arthur."

Chelsea went back to her seat and immediately took off her cap. Then Mary Lynne gave a report about Harriet Tubman, an African-American woman who led the Underground Railroad. This, it turned out, wasn't a real railroad at all, but a series of homes where escaping slaves were hidden and then helped on their way.

Thomas was impressed. Who would've thought a chain of ordinary people could secretly conduct slaves all the way to Canada or other safe places?

Abigail told everyone about the Duchess of Windsor, Wallis Warfield Simpson, who came from Baltimore. Next, Charlie gave his report about Babe Ruth.

"All right," said Mrs. Findlay. "That's everyone." She checked her grade book.

Arthur turned around and whispered to Thomas, "Who do you think's going to get a prize?"

Thomas sighed. "I don't know. I just hope it's

not her." He pointed to Beverly Ann.

"I'm ready to announce the winners." Smiling, Mrs. Findlay stood and said, "First prize goes to . . ."

Thomas crossed his fingers. If Beverly Ann wins—well, he didn't even want to think about it.

"Mary Lynne Woodlie!"

Aaaah. Thomas smiled with relief.

Around the room, there were murmurs of agreement, and then clapping. Mrs. Findlay pinned a large blue ribbon to Mary Lynne's shirt.

Then she said, "Second prize goes to . . . Chelsea Martin!" Beaming, Chelsea put her cap back on her head and went to stand next to Mary Lynne.

While Mrs. Findlay pinned on Chelsea's red ribbon, Thomas heard Beverly Ann muttering under her breath.

"That's not all," said the teacher. "I've decided to give out two additional awards."

She held up a green ribbon. "The prize for the most original report goes to . . . Arthur Wilmot!"

Arthur jumped as if someone had stuck a pin

into him. Then he looked over his shoulder at Thomas and gave him a big smile.

"Yes!" Thomas said.

"The last award is very important," said Mrs. Findlay in a serious voice. "The prize for most improved goes to . . . Thomas Tuttle!"

What! Thomas stared at the teacher. That can't be right, he thought.

He pointed to his chest. "Me?"

Mrs. Findlay smiled. "Yes, you."

Proudly, Thomas went to stand at the front of the room, next to Mary Lynne, Chelsea, and Arthur. Mrs. Findlay pinned a green ribbon to his shirt, too.

Arthur pointed to his own chest. "Wait till my parents see this," he whispered to Thomas.

Thomas said, "I know. My mom and dad are gonna faint when they see mine."

Then Mrs. Findlay got everyone's attention. "I want you to line up now," she said. "We're going to the gymnasium to hear the fifth grade sing 'Maryland, My Maryland.'"

The third graders started milling around the

room, and Thomas passed near Beverly Ann. "Hah!" he said. "I thought you were going to win a prize."

He expected her to make some smart remark. Instead, she turned and walked away.

Thomas stood still. He'd seen tears in her eyes. He was glad Beverly Ann had lost the contest. But he hadn't realized she'd feel that bad about it.

He called across to her. "Beverly Ann, your singing was good!"

She looked surprised. "Oh . . . thanks." With a smile, she smoothed her hair.

Arthur yanked at Thomas's arm. "Hey!" he said as he pulled him aside. "What'd you say that for? Her singing was awful!"

Thomas shook his head and grinned. "It was good, all right," he said softly to Arthur. "Good and *loud*!"

BECKY THOMAN LINDBERG lives in Baltimore, Maryland, with her husband, son, and daughter, as well as a dog and two cats. Besides writing, she enjoys art; she paints landscapes and portraits in oils and pastels.

As a child, Mrs. Lindberg read many books and occasionally wrote stories of her own. *Thomas Tuttle, Just in Time* and the other two books in this series, *Speak Up, Chelsea Martin!* and *Chelsea Martin Turns Green,* were inspired by her childhood memories and by the adventures of her son, Peter, and her daughter, Carolyn.